Based on the screenplay written by Dan Berendsen
Based on characters created by Michael Poryes and Rich Correll & Barry O'Brien
Executive Producers Michael Poryes and Steve Peterman, David Blocker
Produced by Alfred Gough and Miles Millar
Directed by Peter Chelsom

DISNEY PRESS
New York

NOV 0 9

KN

When Miley Stewart was little, she lived in Crowley Corners, Tennessee. Life was simple there. She spent time with friends and family. There was even a boy who had a big crush on her. His name was Travis Brody.

But then Miley and her father and brother moved to California, and everything got complicated. That's when she started her secret life . . . as pop superstar Hannah Montana.

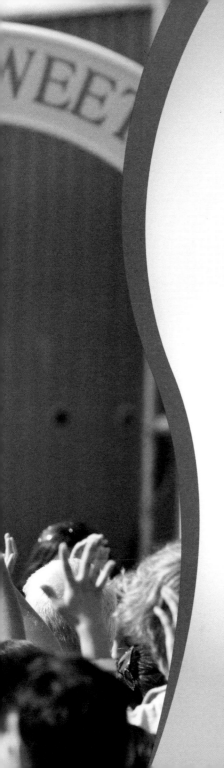

As Hannah, Miley got to sing at sold-out concerts packed with screaming fans.

When Hannah's shows were over, she could go back to being just Miley.

It was the best of both worlds.

But all of a sudden, Miley was having trouble keeping her two lives straight. She forgot to say good-bye to her brother before he left for college because she was shopping for a Hannah event. And she showed up late—dressed as Hannah—to her best friend Lilly Truscott's Sweet Sixteen party.

Miley's father, Robby Ray Stewart, didn't like the way Miley was acting. He thought she was letting a lot of people down. He took her back to Crowley Corners.

Mr. Stewart wanted Miley to take two weeks off from being Hannah. He wanted her to get back in touch with her country roots. But Miley only wanted to get back to California.

"I want to go home!" she cried.

"You *are* home," her father said. "Look around." He climbed into an old pickup truck and left Miley standing there alone in the field.

Miley's old horse, Blue Jeans, was grazing nearby. She tried to climb on his back but fell off when she reached down for her suitcase. Blue Jeans took off running.

Then another horse galloped past!

The rider was a boy about Miley's age. He lassoed Blue Jeans and brought him back over to where Miley was still sitting on the ground.

"Blue Jeans doesn't really take to strangers," he said.
"I know," Miley retorted. "He's my horse."
The boy's eyes widened. "Miley?" he asked. "It's me, Travis."
Miley stared at him. She hadn't seen Travis Brody in years!
He pulled her up onto his horse and gave her a ride home.

The next afternoon, Miley went into town to help out at the farmer's market.

Her Grandma Ruby had a stand selling watermelons. She was trying to raise money to stop developers from paving over part of the town. She didn't want to see it taken over by big new houses and stores and restaurants.

Miley didn't really see what the problem was. As far as she could tell, the town needed some new places to hang out.

Later that day, Miley went out to the barn to practice a song she'd written. She thought she was alone, but as she was singing someone crept up on her. Travis had come to work on the chicken coop!

"Hey, it's great you're still doing that singin' thing," he said. "Everybody knows that's all you ever wanted to do. You actually got a nice voice."

"So, uh, what did you think of that song?" she asked.

"It wasn't bad," said Travis. "It just wasn't . . . about anything. It didn't tell me who you are. What you feel." Travis wasn't trying to be mean. He was just being honest.

Travis went back to fixing the chicken coop. He wanted to start a business selling eggs.

"So that's all you want to do?" Miley asked. "Sell eggs in Crowley Corners?"

"You just don't get this place at all, do you?" Travis shook his head. "Come on. Let's go."

Travis took Miley on a horseback ride. They galloped until they reached a quiet pond surrounded by wildflowers. Suddenly, Miley realized she'd been here before—with Travis. The memories came flooding back.

"Look, there's jumpy rock," she said excitedly. "And the fort used to be over there. Remember? And our swing—"

Travis helped Miley remember what she'd always loved about her hometown. Now she could see why Grandma Ruby wanted to keep it just as it was.

At a fund-raising event to save Crowley Meadows, Travis convinced Miley to sing for the crowd. It felt weird to be onstage as herself and not as Hannah. But she had a lot of fun.

Later, Miley and Travis danced together while other people sang. Miley had a lot of fun spending time with Travis. In fact, she was starting to think *she* had a crush on *him*.

The only problem with the fund-raiser was that it hadn't raised much money at all. Miley had told Travis that she knew Hannah Montana. He spoke up then and suggested that Miley ask the pop star to come give a concert.

When Hannah Montana came to town, everyone was excited to see her.

Travis welcomed Hannah warmly. But all he wanted to talk about was Miley. He decided to ask Miley out on a date!

Miley was so excited!

But she had forgotten that Hannah was supposed to be the mayor's guest at a dinner the same night. Her father left the choice up to her.

The next night, Miley hoped that nobody would notice if she slipped out of the mayor's dinner, changed out of her Hannah outfit into a different dress, and met Travis at the restaurant across the street.

But with all her running back and forth, someone did notice: Travis. He spotted her taking off her Hannah wig.

Miley started to explain, but Travis cut her off. "Explain what? How you've been lying to me this whole time?"

Miley felt terrible.

The next day, when Hannah Montana danced onto the stage at her concert, the crowd went wild. But when she spotted Travis in the audience, she stopped singing. She didn't want to lie anymore. She took off her wig and told the crowd the truth. Then she started to sing the song she'd written. After talking to Travis, she had changed the lyrics. Now the song came from her heart.

Miley had finally learned what was really important . . . and it wasn't being Hannah Montana!

Miley met Travis backstage. She was surprised to find
out that he didn't want her to give up her dream of being a
pop star. He wanted her to be Hannah Montana!

And then Travis kissed her.

Miley was so happy. She was living her dream after all.